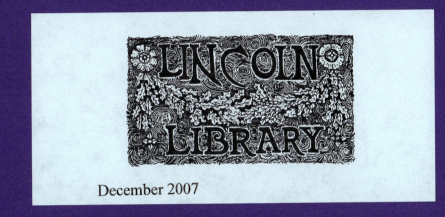

Big Brown Bear's Birthday Surprise

David McPhail

Big Brown Bear's Birthday Surprise

Harcourt, Inc.

Orlando   Austin   New York   San Diego   Toronto   London

www.HarcourtBooks.com

Library of Congress Cataloging-in-Publication Data
McPhail, David, 1940–
Big Brown Bear's birthday surprise/David McPhail.
p.   cm.
Summary: An excited Bear mistakenly believes that Rat has given him a boat for his birthday.
[1. Birthdays—Fiction. 2. Friendship—Fiction. 3. Bears—Fiction. 4. Rats—Fiction.] I. Title.
PZ7.M2427Bg 2007
[E]—dc22   2006004451
ISBN 978-0-15-206098-5

H G F E D C B

Printed in Singapore

The illustrations in this book were done in pen and ink and watercolor.
The display and text type was set in Old Claude.
Color separations by Bright Arts Ltd., Hong Kong
Printed and bound by Tien Wah Press, Singapore
This book was printed on totally chlorine-free Stora Enso Matte paper.
Production supervision by Christine Witnik
Designed by Lauren Rille

For Kofi and his uncles, Pepe and Kiko, with love

One

It was a fine summer day. Big Brown Bear and his friend Rat were having a picnic.

"What a good idea this was, Rat," said Bear. "I do so love a picnic."

"Would you like another cucumber sandwich?" asked Rat. "There is one left."

"I suppose I could eat one more,"
Bear replied. "They are my favorite."

"Yes, I know," said Rat.
"That is why I made ten of them."

"What a special day," said Big Brown Bear.

"Indeed," said Rat. "And do you know why it's so special?"

"Why?" asked Bear.

"Because today is someone's birthday," explained Rat.

"Someone I know?" asked Bear.

"Yes," answered Rat. "Someone you know very well."

"Oh, Rat," cried Big Brown Bear, "it's your birthday!"

"Not mine, Bear," said Rat. "It's yours!"

"Really?" asked Bear. "How do you know?"

"I remembered from last year," said Rat. "Birthdays don't change. They are always on the same day."

"Amazing," said Bear.

Two

Big Brown Bear finished his sandwich,
then lay back on the grass
and closed his eyes.

"Don't go to sleep," said Rat.

"I have a surprise for you."

"What is it?" asked Bear.

"I'll give you a clue," said Rat

as he disappeared into the picnic basket.

"It has four letters and begins with a *B*."

Just then, Big Brown Bear felt something bump the bottom of his foot. He sat up and looked. It was a boat!

"Oh, thank you, Rat!" he cried. "I have always wanted a boat!"

"I didn't get you a boat, Bear,"
said Rat, emerging from the basket.
But when he looked, Bear wasn't there.
He was sitting in the boat, adjusting the oars.
"Jump aboard, Rat," Bear called. "Let's go for a ride!"

Rat saw that the boat was moving away from shore, so he quickly leaped into the seat next to Bear. "As I was saying, Bear," he tried to explain, "this is *not* your boat."

"Whose is it, then?" Bear asked.

"I don't know," said Rat. "It must've gotten loose and drifted downstream."

"Then we'll return it," said Bear. "And have a boat ride, too."

Three

With Bear working one oar
and Rat working the other, the
boat moved steadily up the river.
"Boating is so much fun," said Big Brown Bear.

Just then a hat came floating by.
Bear scooped it up and put it on his head.

Next came a fishing pole. Bear grabbed it and handed his oar to Rat.

"Row on, will you, Rat?" he asked. "I would like to fish."

No sooner had Bear dipped his line into the water than a log drifted into view. And sitting on the log was a man.

"Hullo!" called Bear. "What a fine day to be on the river."

"Without a boot it isn't," the man called back. "Hey...that's my hat you're wearing!"

"If you say so," said Bear. And he tossed the hat to the man.

"That's my fishing pole, too," the man shouted.

"You're welcome to it," said Big Brown Bear. He held it out for the man.

"And that's my boat!" the man yelled.

"We found it downstream," explained Rat,

"and we were trying to return it."

Rat steered over to the log, and Bear helped the man climb into the boat.

"I'm glad you came along when you did," the man told them. "That log was getting tippy."

With the addition of the man, there was hardly any room to row. Even worse, water was pouring in over the sides.

Rat rowed faster. The man began to bail. But the extra weight was too much, and the boat slowly sank.

Once they'd all swum safely to shore, the man decided he'd had enough boating for one day. He was going home.

"Thanks for rescuing me!" he called over his shoulder.

"Anytime!" Bear called back. "Thank *you* for the boat ride."

Four

When the man was out of sight,
Bear and Rat headed back to collect the picnic basket.
As they walked along, Bear remembered something.
"Say, Rat," he said, "this has been a terrific birthday.
But if the boat wasn't my present...
what is?"

"I'm afraid it's not much of a present," said Rat. "Not compared to a boat."

"Oh, boats are all right," said Bear. "But they can sink."

"You're right about that, Bear," said Rat as he reached into the picnic basket.

"Here is your present," he said, and he handed a ball to Bear.

"Oh, Rat!" cried Bear. "What a beautiful ball!"

"Do you really like it?" asked Rat.

"I do indeed," said Bear.

"Watch this!"

He tossed the ball high into the air,
caught it on the tip of his nose,
and balanced it there
all the way home...

...where Rat had another surprise waiting.